TEARS
of a Friend

" 'Maybe I want people to look at me for once! They're always looking at *you*!'

Claire's face goes red. 'Cassie, you're being stupid.'

'Am I?' I shout. 'Is that what you really think of me? Stupid? Well, you know what, Claire? I'm fed up of being your shadow! I'm fed up of not being noticed. I'm out of here!' **"**

SHARP SHADES 2.0

TEARS
of a Friend

More great reads in the
SHARP SHADES 2.0 *series:*

TEARS
of a Friend

HIGHLAND
LIBRARIES

Jo Cotterill

WITHDRAWN

Ransom

SHARP SHADES 2.0
Tears of a Friend
by Jo Cotterill

Published by Ransom Publishing Ltd.
Radley House, 8 St. Cross Road, Winchester, Hampshire SO23 9HX, UK
www.ransom.co.uk

ISBN   978 178127 207 7
First published in 2008

CONTENTS

CHAPTER ONE

My best friend Claire is cross. 'It's not fair. My parents have told me to stay home for *two weeks!*'

Her older brother Nick plays in a band. She went out last night to his gig.

'What time did you get in?' I ask.

'Midnight,' she says. 'It's not even that late! It is so unfair that I'm grounded!'

Claire is fourteen, the same age as me. But we don't look alike at all. She is really pretty, with long, blond hair. I am plain, with hair that always looks a mess.

'Did you meet a boy?' I ask.

She grins. 'What do you think?'

I think that means yes.

The school bell rings. We pick up our bags.

'Did you know Louise is having a party?' says Claire. 'Next Thursday.'

'Cool!' I say. 'But will your parents let you go?'

Claire shrugs her shoulders. 'Who cares? I'm going anyway!' Then she gives a sigh. 'I've got nothing to wear.'

She always says this! Claire has WAY more clothes than I do. But I really *do* need a new outfit.

'I've got nothing to wear either,' I say.

Claire cheers up. 'Let's go shopping!'

CHAPTER TWO

The shopping centre is always busy on a Saturday. There are lots of people here today.

'Over here, Cassie!' Claire calls to me. She looks awesome. Pink crop-top and tight jeans.

'Oh my God!' I gasp. 'Is that a belly-button ring?'

Claire giggles. 'It's a stick-on jewel. Fab, isn't it?'

'It looks really cool,' I say. I want one too. But that would be copying. And Claire always laughs at me if I say I want the same as her.

'Come on, there's some new stuff in H&M.' Claire drags me off.

I love trying on clothes. It's my fave thing ever!

We're in New Look. Claire has got this dress on that looks amazing. (Of course. She looks

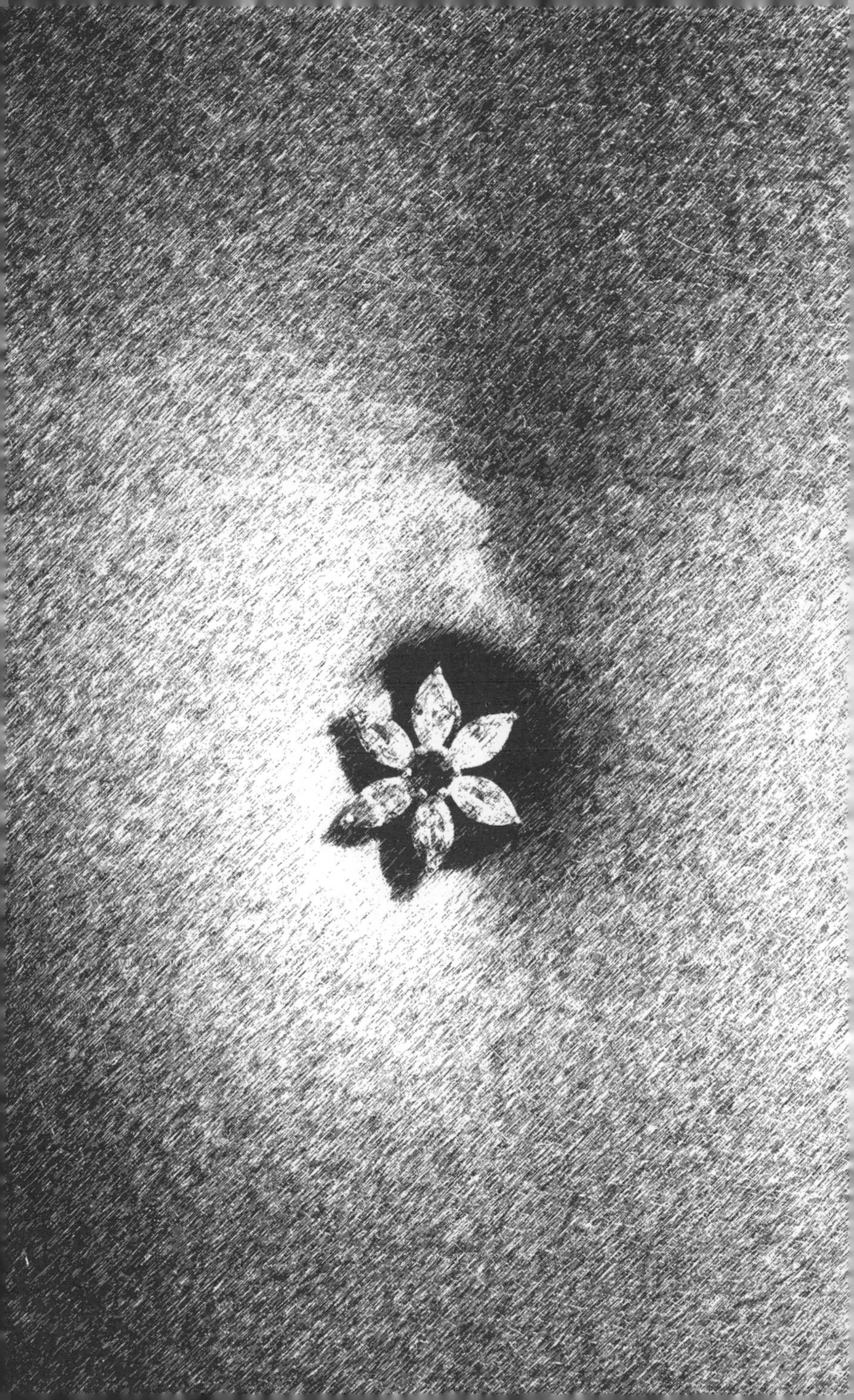

amazing in anything.)

I've put on a dark-green velvet top. I gasp at myself in the mirror. The top is very low cut. I look *fantastic!*

I turn to Claire. 'What do you think?'

'Wait a sec,' she says. 'Do you think this makes me look fat?'

'No,' I say, 'but what about this?'

She doesn't even look at me. 'It's all right.'

I'm suddenly angry. 'Look at me!' I say in a loud voice.

Claire frowns. 'It's nice. But it's not very *you*, is it?'

'What do you mean?' I ask.

'It's not the sort of thing you wear,' Claire says with a shrug. 'It will make people look at you – if that's what you want.'

I am really mad now.

'Maybe I want people to look at me for once! Maybe I'm fed up with people *not* looking at me! They're always looking at *you*!'

Claire's face goes red. 'Cassie, you're being stupid.'

'Am I?' I shout. 'Is that what you really think of me? Stupid? Well, you know what, Claire? I'm fed up of being your shadow! I'm fed up of not being noticed. I'm out of here!'

As I pull the green top over my head I hear something rip. I don't care. I walk really fast out of the shop. I leave Claire behind.

At first I feel proud. I stood up for myself!

But when I get home I burst into tears. I'm not angry any more, just sad. Claire has been my best friend since for ever. Is it all over?

CHAPTER THREE

Monday at school is awful. Claire and I were best friends. I don't have anyone else to hang around with. So I'm on my own all the time.

I have to talk to someone, so I

make friends with Isabel, the nerdy girl in the class. She's so grateful someone wants to be friends. It makes me feel sorry for her, but it annoys me too. I wish she'd stand up for herself a bit.

My mum knows something is wrong. 'Where's Claire these days?' she says.

'We're not friends any more,' I say.

Maybe I'm looking at this the wrong way. Maybe being without Claire is a *good* thing. Maybe it's time for a change. A change in me. It's time to stop being a shadow.

I go back to New Look and buy the green velvet top. Watch out, world! The new Cassie is on her way!

Chapter Four

On the night of the party I feel
nervous. I nearly decide not to go.
But then I feel cross with myself.
There will be lots of people I know
there. I can show them the new me!

I pull on the green top, a short skirt and my heels. I'm not very good at make-up, so I spend a long time doing it.

I try to make my hair look nice, but I use too much hair gel and it feels stiff and horrid.

'You look nice,' says my mum.

'Thanks,' I say, but I still feel nervous. Chin up, I tell myself. I'm trying to be the new Cassie, but it's hard to remember!

Mum shakes her head. 'I can't believe there's a party on a school night. Take your coat, it's cold.'

No way am I wearing my school

coat to the party! 'I'll be fine,' I say.

She grumbles a bit. 'Be back by eleven, OK? And get someone to walk you home, or call me.'

'Yes, Mum.'

I set off to the party. It's not far, but it is *freezing* outside! I wish I'd put on my coat now!

CHAPTER FIVE

A boy opens the door. I don't know him.

'Hi,' he says. His eyes are kind of red. 'Come in.'

I step into the hall. There's loud

music coming from the front room, and a big crowd. Where should I go?

I don't see anyone I know. Most people seem a lot older than me.

Then my heart stops. It's Nick, Claire's brother. He's wearing a leather jacket and holding a bottle of beer. He looks *amazing*.

'Hi,' I shout over the music, 'I'm Cassie, Claire's friend.'

Nick turns to look at me, and then I do something really stupid. I put my hand out to shake hands!

'Oh yeah, hi,' he says. I don't think he remembers me. I pull back my hand. I hope I don't look too dumb.

'How are you?' I say. 'I hear your gig went really well last week.'

Nick stares at me.

'Yeah, it was cool.' He takes a swig from the beer bottle. His eyes slide down. 'Nice top,' he says. Then he goes into the front room.

All of a sudden I'm not sure about my top. I should feel pleased that Nick liked it, but I feel a bit dirty. I didn't like the way he looked at me.

All in all, talking to Nick didn't go very well. I go to the kitchen in the hope of finding a friend.

I bump into a couple snogging by the stairs. 'Sorry,' I say.

'Look out,' snaps the girl. It's Claire. Her eyes open wide when she sees me. But then she starts kissing the boy again. It's not someone I know. I go past them, feeling sick.

The kitchen is buzzing. There's a funny smell in the air too, like Mum's musk perfume. I pour myself a Coke and feel grumpy. Why did I come?

'Hiya, sexy.' A boy is gazing at me. He looks about eighteen, and his eyes are fixed on my boobs. This top was totally a mistake. 'Want to have a bit of fun?' He shows me a plastic bag. What's it got inside?

Leaves? No – drugs!

'No thank you,' I say in a squeak.

'Go on. You look like the kind of girl who needs to relax.'

He's very tall and is leaning over me.

'No,' I say.

He reaches out a hand to my chest. I can't move!

'Hiya, Cassie,' says a cheerful voice from somewhere near. 'Do you want some fresh air?' And a hand grabs mine and pulls me away.

CHAPTER SIX

When we're out of the kitchen I see who saved me.

'Mark!' I say. He's in my maths class at school, but I don't know him that well.

'You looked like you needed help,' he says, letting go of my hand. 'Hope I did the right thing.'

'Yeah, thanks,' I say.

'Do you want to go outside? You don't have to,' says Mark.

'No, I'd like to,' I say. 'It's too hot in here.'

As we head out the front door, we pass a couple going up the stairs.

'Isn't that your friend Claire?' Mark says.

Claire is giggling. The guy she was snogging has his hand on her bum. Her skirt is up around her

waist. I hope she knows what she's doing.

I follow Mark into the front garden. It's really cold out here!

Mark says, 'Hang on,' and goes back into the house. He comes out with two winter coats.

'Where did you get them?' I ask.

He grins. 'They were by the front door. Don't worry, we'll just borrow them.'

I laugh. 'Thanks!' Once the coat is on, I feel a lot warmer.

Mark sits down next to me and now I feel nervous. He got me a coat. Does he want to kiss me? Or was he just being nice?

All of a sudden, Mark says, 'I hate parties. Everyone is stupid at a party. If you're not getting drunk, people think you're weird.'

'I know what you mean!' I say, glad that he feels the same way as me. 'Why do people drink so much? It only makes you sick! Why is that fun?'

'It's not,' said Mark. 'But we must be the only two here who think that!'

We smile at each other.

'I'm glad we came out here,' I say.

'Me too.'

CHAPTER SEVEN

After that we have a good chat. It's nice. I don't have any friends that are boys but Mark's OK. He doesn't try to kiss me. We talk about school, friends, family. I even tell him about my row with Claire.

Then there's a shout from the front door. A girl runs out. Her make-up is all messed up and she's got no shoes on. She's crying.

It's Claire!

I go to help her. 'Claire, what's the matter?'

She screams at me. 'Get off me, get off me!' Then she runs off.

I'm worried. 'I should do something,' I say to Mark.

'She'll be home soon,' he says. 'I'm sure she'll be OK.'

I really hope so.

CHAPTER EIGHT

Mark walks me home. Mum likes the look of him, I can tell. 'Won't you come in for coffee?' she asks.

I'm glad that Mark says no. I don't want Mum asking him all

about the party!

Mark waves at me. 'See you tomorrow, Cassie.'

'Yeah. Thanks again,' I say.

It takes me a long time to go to sleep. I keep thinking about Claire. I hope she got home OK. I send her a text but there's no reply.

She's not at school the next day. It worries me so much that I go to her house after school.

Claire's dad opens the door. He works from home. He smiles at me. 'Hi, Cassie. Have you come to see Claire?' He looks cross now. 'She's in big trouble. She went to a party last night and we told her not to.'

'Oh, really?' I say.

'Yes. Maybe you can find out what's going on with her,' he says. 'Go on up. She's just got home from school.'

He doesn't know she wasn't at school today! I don't tell him.

I go up and knock on Claire's bedroom door. 'Claire? It's me.'

'Come in,' she says in a soft voice.

When I go in I see her lying on her bed. She's wearing her school uniform.

'Are you OK?' I ask. 'I was worried when you weren't at school.'

'Don't tell Dad!' she says.

'I won't!' I say. 'But what's going on?'

'Why do you care?' She gives me an angry look. 'You hate being my shadow, remember?'

'I still do,' I say. 'But I was worried about you. If you don't want to talk, maybe I'll go.'

'No, Cassie, wait!' Claire reaches out a hand. 'Stay. Please.'

I look at her. 'Go on then. What happened at the party?'

She takes a deep breath. 'That boy tried to make me have sex with him.'

CHAPTER NINE

'*What?*' I say. 'Oh my God, are you OK?'

'I'm all right,' says Claire. 'It didn't happen.'

'Tell me from the start,' I say.

'Well, you saw me with him,'

Claire says. I nod. 'He was really nice, and he said he liked me. I didn't have anyone else to talk to.'

'I know how you felt,' I say.

'He said he was seventeen, Cassie! He was so fit!' Claire's face goes red. 'I told him I was sixteen.'

'*Claire!*'

She says, 'I knew he wouldn't want me if I told him the truth. He was really good at kissing. And he gave me a drink, but I think he put something in it. It made me laugh. And then he took me upstairs.'

'Why didn't you say something?' I ask.

Claire shakes her head. 'I don't know. I think I was too drunk. I fell on a bed and he fell on top of me. And then he put his hand up my skirt.'

'What did you do?' I ask.

Claire has tears in her eyes. 'I didn't know *what* to do. I felt like maybe I should let him, you know. Because I had been kissing him. I led him on, didn't I? But I didn't like it. And so I said STOP and he got mad at me.'

I grab her hand and hold it. 'You poor thing.'

'He yelled at me,' says Claire. 'He

said boys can't stop once they start.'

'That's not true,' I say. 'You can say no at any time.'

'He held me down,' says Claire. 'And I tried to fight him but he was so strong!' Tears run down her cheeks. 'And then Louise came in.'

CHAPTER TEN

'*Louise?*' I say.

'Yeah,' Claire gives a little smile.
'She was yelling at us. We were in
her parents' room!'

I let out a giggle. I can't help it.

'What did the boy say?'

'Nothing,' Claire says. 'He was looking for his pants.'

I giggle even more. 'His pants?'

'I ran out. Last I saw, Louise was hitting him on the head with a tissue box.'

We look at each other and laugh. What a crazy thing to happen!

When we stop laughing, I ask, 'Are you going to tell anyone?'

'Like who?'

'The police?' I say. 'Your parents?'

Claire sits up. 'Are you mad? After the fuss they made last night?'

'He might do it again,' I say. 'To

someone else.'

Claire thinks. 'No. It must have been me. I got myself into that mess.'

I look at her, but I don't know what to say. I don't think it was her fault, but other people may think it. She did wear a short skirt. And she did kiss that boy. But that didn't mean she wanted sex. 'You told him to stop,' I say. 'It's not your fault.'

'It doesn't matter now,' says Claire. 'I was drunk. I made a mistake. I'll know better next time.'

I don't say anything.

'So, what about you?' Claire asks.

'Did you have a good time at the party?'

I grin. 'I met this boy ... '

'Cassie!'

'It's OK,' I say. 'You know him. Mark from our class?'

'Mark? From maths?'

'Yeah. He saved me from a creep who tried to give me drugs.'

Claire's eyes open wide. 'Drugs?'

I giggle. 'I know. I was so freaked out I nearly said yes.'

Claire grabs my arms. 'Who are you? What have you done with Cassie?' she jokes.

We burst out laughing again. All

the hurt from the last week is going away.

'I missed you,' I say to Claire.

'No you didn't,' she says. 'You had *Isabel*.'

'She's not like you,' I say.

Claire laughs. 'Thank God! Did you see what she was wearing at the party?'

'I know.'

'You looked nice,' Claire goes on. 'I liked that green top you wore.'

I can't believe it. Doesn't she remember our shopping trip? 'You didn't like it last time,' I say.

'Last time?' Claire stares at me. 'I

haven't seen it before.'

'Yes, you have. I tried it on in New Look. You were there.'

She shakes her head. 'I don't remember.'

I feel cross. This is something I don't like about Claire. She doesn't know what's important to me!

But we've fallen out before. And I hated it. I don't want to lose my friend again.

I try to smile. 'It doesn't matter,' I say. 'You want to go out tomorrow?'

'Where?' asks Claire. 'Shopping?'

'Will your parents let you go?' I ask. 'Are they still mad?'

'I'll talk to them,' says Claire. 'I think I need to say sorry about the party.'

'OK,' I say. 'Sounds good. Shall we go to see a film?'

Claire shakes her head. 'There's nothing good on. What about bowling?'

'No,' I say. 'The floor squeaks. It makes me feel ill!'

'Cassie, you're such a wuss.'

'Shall we swim?' I ask.

Claire lets out a little scream. 'Are you crazy? Have you *seen* how white I am right now? I'm not going to wear a bikini until I've had my tan

done. You'd better let *me* choose
what we'll do.'

I sigh. Some things never change!

Witness

by Anne Cassidy

Todd sees his ex-teacher Jason Ripley attacking a shopkeeper he knows from his paper round. He is shocked by what he has witnessed, so Todd informs the police. But Todd has no idea just how this will change his life.

Shouting at the Stars

by David Belbin

For singer Layla it's all a dream come true. Her first album hits the big time and her concerts are all sold out. But a heckler starts to show up at her gigs and quickly turns everything into a nightmare.

Blitz

by David Orme

During World War Two Martin is evacuated to Winchester. He hates it there, so travels back home to London. But a bomb has destroyed his house. What future is there for Martin, homeless in a city at war?

Plague

by David Orme

It is 1665 and the plague has hit the city of London. Life will never be the same again for Henry Harper. His father is dead and his mother and brother have fled. Can Henry escape before the plague strikes him?

Wrong Exit

by Mary Chapman

When their mum wanders off in the fog to look for petrol, Grace Adam and Ruby wait in the car. Suddenly they enter a strange, terrible, new world. Nothing is quite as it should be. Did they take a wrong exit?

The Messenger

by John Townsend

Chris sees a Christmas glass angel smash at his feet. Then a trip to the moors with his girlfriend brings strange events. They even seem to be moving in time. What connects past, present and future?

Hunter's Moon

by John Townsend

Neil is a young gamekeeper, left to look after the woods on his own. There are rumours of a panther on the loose, and now Neil notices odd scratch marks on the trees. Will Neil take action before it is too late?

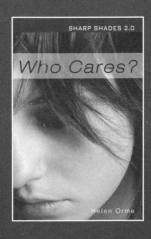

Who Cares?

by Helen Orme

Tara hates her life and everyone around her. Most of all, she hates her special school, the Unit. Then she meets Liam. Things start to get better, but he wants Tara to kick her drug habit. Can she? Will she?

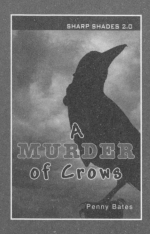

A Murder of Crows

by Penny Bates

Only-child Ben moves to the country with his mum. Soon he is friends with a crow. This makes Ben a laughing stock. The bullies want him to hurt the thing he loves the most. But no one must forget Crow Law!

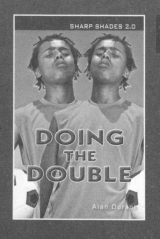

Doing the Double

by Alan Durant

Footballing twins Dale and Joe have always joked about swapping their identities for a day. Now Dale wants Joe to do the double and take his place on the football pitch – for real. How can Joe refuse his twin?